D1396647

THIS BOOK BELONGS TO

Nari ☺

WHEN I GROW UP I WANT TO BE...

Text and Illustrations copyright © 2020 by Delanda Coleman and Terrence Coleman

All rights reserved. No part of this publication may be reproduced, distributed, or transmitted in any form or by any means, including photocopying, recording, or other electronic or mechanical methods, without the prior written permission of the publisher, except in the case of brief quotations embodied in reviews and certain other non-commercial uses permitted by copyright law. The moral right of the author and illustrator has been asserted.

Cover design and illustrations by Beatriz Mello

Published by Sydney and Coleman, LLC
Boston, Massachusetts

PARENT GUIDE

Hi Parents - Thank you for purchasing the More Than a Princess activity and coloring book!

This book is meant to be an optional companion to the More Than a Princess book, which is available at Amazon.com. We developed this book to be fun AND educational. The activities are designed to give your child more exposure to the areas of science, technology, engineering, art, and math (STEAM) and to also encourage them to explore potential careers as either an astronaut, doctor, engineer, or artist.

Types of activities

- **Drawing and writing prompts:** Writing and drawing prompts are designed to get your child interested in specific topics while encouraging them to write and draw about them in a thoughtful and imaginative way. Combined with journaling, these prompts are ideal for helping children express their feelings and establish new ideas.
- **Mazes:** Solving mazes boosts patience and persistence and teaches kids about the rewards of hard work. Mazes can also help improve a child's cognitive thought processes. Solving and concentrating on mazes help improve hand-eye coordination memory.
- **Word searches & crossword puzzles:** Word searches and crossword puzzles are designed to accompany the More Than a Princess story. They can assist in spelling, word recognition and build language fluency, the ability to read with speed, accuracy, and proper expression. They also help to develop pattern recognition. For example, how the letter Q is usually followed by the letter U.

Timing & structuring activities

We recommend spending 20 minutes to an hour each day applying activities from this book. Although each child is unique, children in 1st grade or higher should target for about an hour of activities. Consider spending every day reinforcing creative writing and drawing. This will help your child improve communication skills, retain what they have learned and encourage creativity and exploration.

Some words in this book may be challenging for younger children. That's OK. These words are intentionally designed to push them a little harder. We recommend embracing the technology you have around you. For example, if you have Alexa, Siri, or Google-enabled devices, ask your child to ask the devices to define the complex words. Your child will be utilizing technology to support their learning. Also, you will be given opportunities to have more complex discussions about what they have learned.

Kiana is more than a princess and our children are more than exceptional! These strategies have been tested with our daughter and niece. As a result, they have learned many techniques that will help them for years to come!

We hope you enjoy!

Delanda & Terrence Coleman
Founders of Sydney and Coleman LLC

PRINCESS KIANA.

List all the things you could do for fun with Princess Kiana?

☑ _____

☑ _____

☑ _____

☑ _____

☑ _____

☑ _____

☑ _____

☑ _____

☑ _____

☑ _____

☑ _____

☑ _____

☑ _____

☑ _____

☑ _____

If you could learn about anything, what would it be?

MEDICINE

DESIGN

MATH

ENGINEERING

PRINCESS KIANA.

What is Kiana reading about? Write a story about all the things Kiana is learning in the book.

_____

_____

_____

_____

_____

_____

_____

_____

_____

_____

_____

_____

_____

Draw a picture of planets and stars in outer space.

CAPTAIN KIANA.

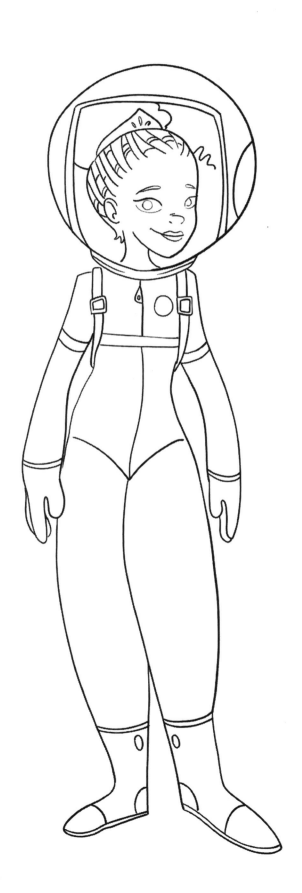

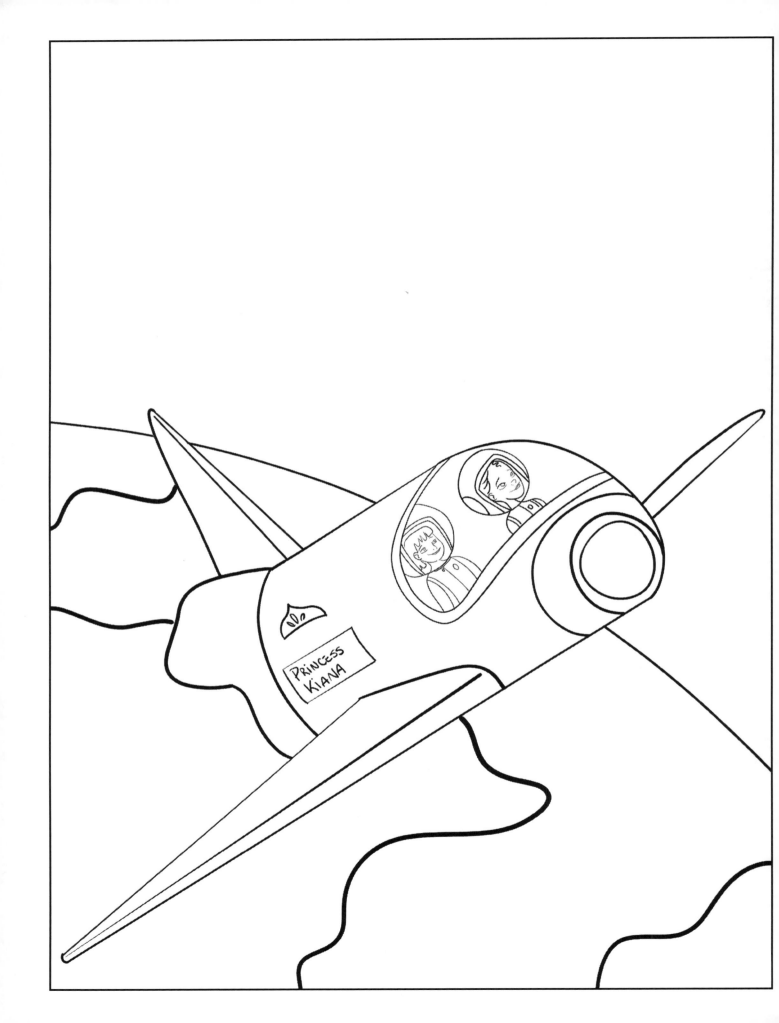

Draw a picture of all the items Kiana uses on her patients.

Hints:

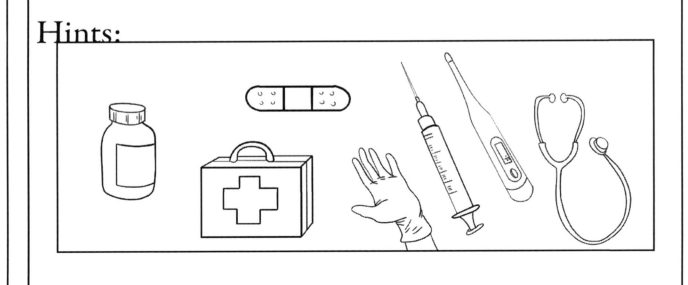

DOCTOR KIANA.

Help the nurse and her patient find their way to the hospital.

Draw a picture of a robot that helps you clean your room.

ENGINEER KIANA.

Circle each word from the list in the puzzle.

Word Search

```
p a m t o e y p a c t p f o e
q r c o e x p l o r e o c s a
r l i l o n j s c e f q a a r
o h i n c c s s a v r s k t t
b g e e c o m q s g m p i e i
o o n j t e d j t y a a a l s
t d g w b m s u r l r c n l t
j m i c d e g s o z s e a i k
s o n a e d k g n l p s r t f
g t e s s i b s a s c h f e z
y h e t i c b v u z v i x k y
p e r l g i o p t u a p z k f
k r t e n n n d o c t o r x v
v j r a y e e j x g i q j p l
r d i t p d s g b u i l d e r
```

astronaut	satellite	godmother
medicine	engineer	space ship
builder	artist	doctor
Kiana	design	bones
mars	princess	explore
castle	robot	

Draw a picture of a place you can explore with Kiana.

ARTIST KIANA.

What should Kiana draw?
Draw a picture of your favorite thing to do.

Design a space ship on the computer screen.

JOURNAL ENTRY

Chose a dream job when you grow up. Write a
journal entry about a typical day on the job.

A SMART PRINCESS.

WRITE A LETTER

Write a letter to yourself when you are all grown up.
What advice would you give yourself about school?

Image your self all grown up. Draw your picture of yourself in the frame on the desk and write your name on the diploma.

DIPLOMA

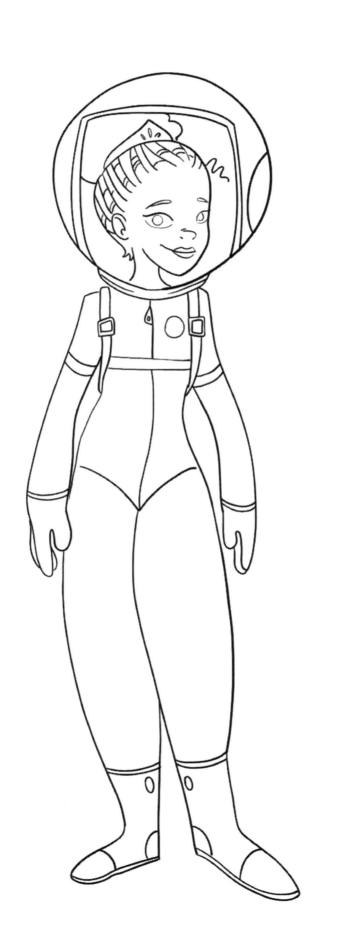

Help Kiana find her way to the library.

Circle each word from the list in the puzzle.

Doctor

```
I E W P M U H B W M E Y L I B
V P T A E E A W F E C J H Y R
D T J U Y D D B O N E S K G A
L D H S P L I I I H K B J G I
D O K Q T J H A C S X G B Z N
M C F O C E H E T I I U W T U
T T J P T A T O A R N H D I Y
T O X D F Y D H S L I E Z C G
P R Y A C R I E O P T C C U I
X H K B C B I N N S I H I E K
P E I B G P A U S T C T G A O
M A A W M A T R O D I O A K N
J R N W F H V S U M F S P L Q
N T A S U R G E O N Q G T E P
J Y F I B N Y M V L M C X P P
```

Pediatrician	Stethoscope	Hospital
Surgeon	Doctor	Health
Bones	Nurse	Heart
Brain	Medicine	Dentist
Kiana		

Circle each word from the list in the puzzle.

Engineer

```
U C E J H P H Y S I C I S T Y
R O B O T S J N Y T G R E W W
O D H E N T R E P R E N E U R
A E W T C H E M I S T E U T J
S C I E N T I S T C M S C E S
I Z V V P D E S I G N H O C L
A N M Z Z R H D W T B A M H M
R F V D I N O M S U V C P N A
C O O E Z L Z G A Q K K U O T
H N Q B N E Y K R C V E T L H
I L W D Z T V O F A H R E O H
T Q V D M T O Z E M M I R G J
E N G I N E E R G E L M N Y G
C Z E Z Y W Q Y H A C I E E W
T X E T K R S U R V Q A X R S
```

entrepreneur	programmer	technology
Engineer	physicist	computer
chemist	design	robots
math	architect	hacker
scientist	inventor	machines
code		

Let's Visit the Hospital

Down:
1. a person who gives you medicine
4. a person who tries to heal patients
6. a medical professional that supports a doctor
7. a skeleton is made up of this

Across:
2. when you are not sick and have no injuries
3. a place you go when you are very sick
5. a doctor that treats children
8. a doctor that looks at your teeth
9. a medical doctor qualified to practice surgery
10. something the doctors give you to feel better

Circle each word from the list in the puzzle.

Artist

```
W A L I N N L Y C T X T E W S
R P E S C U L P T U R E S L K
I V H R R I D E S I G N E R I
T R G O A E D K Y F K F H C A
E M J T T N Q K U T K O A R N
R P Z N U O I X D K Q L R E A
A T I T Y B G M T M I M T A R
P M X F H W L R A T O C I T T
A I L L U S T R A T O R S O D
I C K H P M K N B P O J T R E
N O K L H O L L A L H R G P S
T L M T M V V H V G N E Y H I
E O R G I E D K R R I L R O G
R R X F Z D R A W I N G N X N
V S K T P R L P F Z P W S P A
```

photographer	illustrator	sculpture
animator	artist	painter
art	creator	colors
design	Kiana	designer
Drawing	writer	

Help Princess Kiana un-scramble the following words.

Word Scramble

ATTURSOAN   _____

ELATTILSE   _____

GTDMEOHRO   _____

IRPECNSS   _____

ECMINEID   _____

EENIENGR   _____

PSCEA HSPI   _____

LXEOERP   _____

BLIDEUR   _____

TIASTR   _____

OTORDC   _____

ELATCS   _____

KNAIA   _____

DIENSG   _____

OBSEN   _____

ORTOB   _____

ARSM   _____

Use the following words as a clue.

Artist	astronaut	bones	builder	castle	design
doctor	engineer	explore	godmother	Kiana	mars
medicine	princess	robot	satellite	space ship	

ANSWER KEY

ANSWER KEY

Maze 1

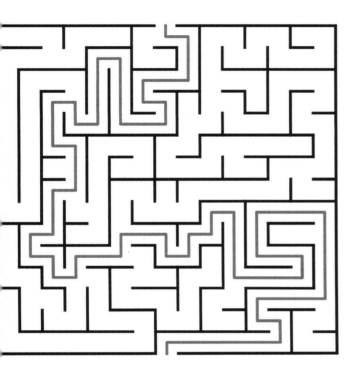

Maze 2

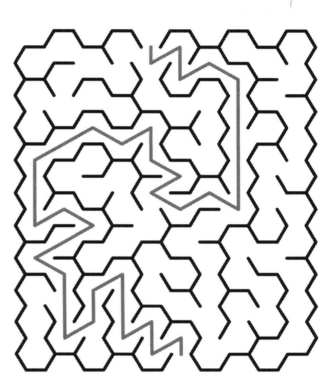

ANSWER KEY

Word Search

```
p a m t o e y p a c t p f o e
q r c o e x p l o r e o c s a
r l i l o n j s c e f q a t r
o h i n c c s s a v r s k i t
b g e e c o m q s g m p a l i
o d g e n j t e d j t y a i s
t o w b m s u s t r l a n a t
j m c d e g s o z l s e s k f
s o a e d k g n s a p s h z
g t s d i b u z v i x k y
y h r l g n p t u a p z k f
p e i g n e d o c t o r x v
k r t a y e j x g i q j p l
v j r a y e s g b u i l d e r
r d i t p d                       
```

astronaut · satellite · godmother · princess
medicine · engineer · space ship · explore
builder · artist · doctor · castle
Kiana · design · bones · robot
mars

Doctor

```
I E W P M U H B W M E Y L I B
V P T A E E A W F E C J H Y R
D T J U Y D D B O N E S K G A
L D H S P L I I H K B J G I
D O K Q T J H A C S X G B Z N
M C F O C E H E T I I U W T U
T T J P T A T O A R N H D I Y
T O X D F Y D H S L I E Z C G
P R Y A C R I F O P T C C U I
X H K B C B I N N S I H I E K
P E I B G P A U S T C T G A O
M A W M A T R O D I O A K N
J R N W F H V S U M F S P L Q
N T A S U R G E O N Q G T E P
J Y F I B N Y M V L M C X P P
```

Pediatrician · Stethoscope · Hospital · Medicine
Surgeon · Doctor · Health · Dentist
Bones · Nurse · Heart · Kiana
Brain

Engineer

```
U C E J H P H Y S I C I S T Y
R O B O T S J N Y T G R E W W
O D H E N T R E P R E N E U R
A E W T C H E M I S T E U T J
S C I E N T I S T C M S C E S
I Z V V P D E S I G N H O C L
A N M Z Z R H D W T B A M H O
R F V D I N O M S U V C P N M
C O O E Z L Z G A Q K K E O A
H N Q B N E Y K R C V E T L T
I L W D Z T V O F A H R G L H
T Q V D M T O Z E M M I R O J
F E N G I N E E R G E L M N Y G
C Z E Z Y W Q Y H A C I E E W
T X E T K R S U R V Q A X R S
```

entrepreneur · programmer · technology · scientist
Engineer · physicist · computer · inventor
chemist · design · robots · machines
math · architect · hacker · code

Artist

```
W A L I N N L Y C T X T E W S
R P E S C U L P T U R E S L K
I T H R R I D E S I G N E R I
T R G O A E D K Y F K F H C A
E M J T T N Q K U T K O A R N
P Z N U O I X D K Q L R I R A
A T I T Y B G M T M I M T R
P M X F H W L R A T O C I S T
A I L L U S T R A T O R S T
I C K H P M K N B P O J R D
N O K L H O L L A L H R G P E
T L M T M V V H V G N E Y H S
E O R G I E D K R R I L R O I
R R X F Z D R A W I N G N X G
V S K T P R L P F Z P W S P A
```

photographer · illustrator · sculpture · designer
animator · artist · painter · Drawing
art · creator · colors · writer
design · Kiana

ANSWER KEY

Let's Visit the Hospital

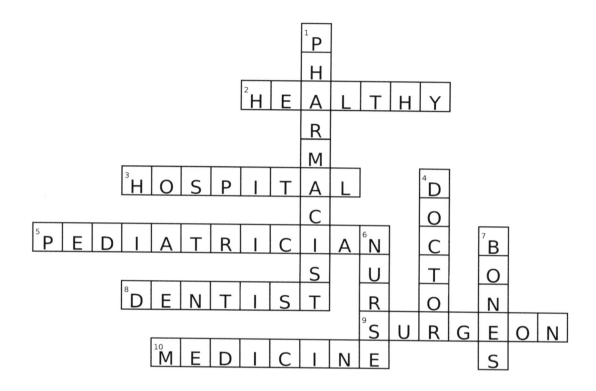

Down:

1. a person who gives you medicine
4. a person who tries to heal patients
6. a medical professional that supports a doctor
7. a skeleton is made up of this

Across:

2. when you are not sick and have no injuries
3. a place you go when you are very sick
5. a doctor that treats children
8. a doctor that looks at your teeth
9. a medical doctor qualified to practice surgery
10. something the doctors give you to feel better

Made in United States
Orlando, FL
24 April 2022

17151331R00024